Snowflake Hollow - Part 12

12 Days of Christmas, Volume 12

Lexy Timms

Published by Dark Shadow Publishing, 2021.

This is a work of fiction. Similarities to real people, places, or events are entirely coincidental.

SNOWFLAKE HOLLOW - PART 12

First edition. December 9, 2021.

Copyright © 2021 Lexy Timms.

Written by Lexy Timms.

Snowflake HOLLOW

12 DAYS OF CHRISTMAS
~PART TWELVE~

USA TODAY BESTSELLING AUTHOR

LEXY TIMMS

Snowflake
HOLLOW
12 DAYS OF CHRISTMAS
PART TWELVE
USA TODAY BESTSELLING AUTHOR
LEXY TIMMS

---

12 Days of Christmas Series

Find Lexy Timms:

LEXY TIMMS NEWSLETTER:

https://www.lexytimms.com/newsletter

Lexy Timms Facebook Page:

https://www.facebook.com/SavingForever

Lexy Timms Website:

http://www.lexytimms.com

Want to read more...
For **FREE?**
Sign up for Lexy Timms' newsletter
And she'll send you updates on new releases, ARC copies of books and
a whole lotta fun!
Sign up for news and updates!
https://www.lexytimms.com/newsletter

Snow Flake Hollow

SPREAD JOY AND LOVE, it's the Christmas season!

She's not the biggest fan of Christmas – which is akin to a major sin in the little town of Snowflake Hollow. And with a name like Holly White, it's fitting that she owns the only B&B in town. The whole season is a huge deal, and the people coming to stay at the B&B are paying a premium to get the ultimate festive experience. She's trying to keep the guests busy, but Hank the Handyman just broke his leg trying to hang the lights. Now she has to figure out how to make the holiday festivities happen all by herself.

Enter Lawson Lane.

Mister tall, dark and handsome, has come home to see his mother over the holidays, and is surprised to see Holly as the owner of the B&B. When he notices her struggling to get things done, he offers a helping hand. Seeing Holly again and enjoying the holidays might take a Christmas miracle—or he might end up with a lump of coal in his stocking.

It's 12 days of festive fun, what could possibly go wrong?

Lexy Timms brings you a Christmas holiday romance with 12 days of Christmas – each part of the story releasing like opening an advent calendar! Join in the holiday spirit with a festive read and some laughs to get you into the Christmas season.

Chapter Sixty-Six

L awson
    I did not mean to say that.

I did not mean to say that.

It just popped out. Like it had been waiting on the edge of my tongue, searching for the first opportunity to leap and make my life a complicated mess. As delicately as I was trying to play all this, and as difficult as our situation was, I felt like I had been doing a great job of remaining cool. Then I had to go and do that.

It's just a phrase, though. Something you say to a friend when you're happy about something that happened. That's what I tried to tell myself, over and over. It didn't mean anything. It was just a phrase. It was clearly just a spur of the moment saying.

But I knew it wasn't true.

It might be crazy, but I knew that those words coming out of my mouth wasn't purely an accident. She had woven herself into my life to such a degree that there was no denying that I had feelings for her. Deep feelings. I was falling in love with her every single day, spiraling further and further into a situation where I knew it was going to come out sooner or later. But I thought I would have more control over it. I would be able to dictate when and how I would approach it.

Then I just blurted it out.

There had to be a right time to discuss it, a time where we could sit down apart from all the craziness of the holiday and talk about what we were to each other. How we were going to continue from here. There was a way of approaching this with maturity and clarity that would keep us both from doing anything we would regret, or rushing headlong into something that one or both of us wasn't ready for.

As we got back into the car to head back to the bed and breakfast, I mentally kicked myself for being so impulsive. I had to be better than that. Turning the key I almost opened my mouth to talk about it, to say something about how I didn't mean it that way. But that would have just made it worse, and I snapped my mouth shut at the last second.

The snow was getting heavier as I pulled onto the road, cursing the fact that we had to go so far to find the toy and now had to drive through the snow. Part of the reason I chose the bed and breakfast in the first place was that it required very little driving to get to things. I wanted to remove that as an obstacle while I was there. There was nothing more annoying than driving in the snow.

But there I was, pushing slowly along the stretch of road that looped around Snowflake Hollow along its edges but was the quickest way from one edge of town to the west to the other on the east where the bed and breakfast was. I could have gone straight through the heart of the city, but the number of traffic lights and Christmas events would have made for a much slower go. At least theoretically.

Now that I was cruising at a neck-breaking speed of fifteen miles an hour, I was growing increasingly convinced that it would have been better that way. At least then there would be people. As it stood, there was nothing but a long, dark road, and snowfall making it difficult to see.

Holly say in the passenger seat, working on crocheting in the light of the snow. Even with snow falling heavily, the moonlight and occasional street light reflected off what was already on the ground and gave off tons of light. If only I could see through the heavy fall from the sky, I could make it back. But as it stood it was getting harder and harder to see, and with no one else on the road I was starting to wonder if it was safe to continue.

We made it a few more minutes before the visibility went completely and I pulled off as much as I could onto the shoulder. Holly looked up nervously from her crocheting and I smiled wanly. I wanted to leave the engine running just to keep the heat on, but we were getting low on gas. Still, I decided to risk it for a few minutes in hopes the storm would move quickly.

"This is way worse than the forecast said it would be," Holly said. "They were calling for maybe a couple of inches."

"This is going to be more than a couple of inches," I muttered. "I just hope it's a fast-moving storm."

I pulled open my phone and looked for a weather forecast. Some of them still had the area only getting a couple inches like before, but others just said 'snow'. As if I couldn't see that. There was no guess as to when it would stop or how much it would dump on us in the meantime. After about ten minutes I looked over at Holly, who had made some impressive progress on her project.

"I think I am going to have to shut the engine off," I said. "We're getting low enough on gas that I want to make sure it can make it back to the house."

"Okay," she said. "It's pretty warm in here right now. And we have those blankets in the backseat."

I had forgotten about the blankets, an idea Holly had before we headed out. Her thought was that if we got stuck in traffic or something, it might be nice to have a blanket so she could take a nap if she needed. Now it was looking like it might be what kept her warm in the cold.

Holly put her crocheting down for a moment and fished in the back for the two blankets, handing one to me and putting the other over her lap. Once they were in place, I shut off the engine and we waited.

The snow didn't stop. An hour or so had gone by, and all that happened was more snow piled onto the hood of the car. The heat from the engine had mostly died away, and we were pulling the blankets tighter and tighter over our bodies. My biggest concern was that we would get stuck, and now it was looking like stopping might have made that situation even worse than if I had tried to push through. Reluctantly, I sat up fully and put my foot on the brake.

I turned the key.

The car didn't start.

"Uh-oh," I muttered.

I tried again, and again the engine tried to turn over but couldn't. It wouldn't start. We were stuck, and in a mountain of snowfall.

"Hmm," Holly said as I sat back in my seat, clearly frustrated. "So, the car won't start back up and we're how many miles from the house?"

"I don't know exactly, but I'd put it at least ten miles," I said. "At least."

"So. No walking then," she said.

I huffed a laugh and shook my head.

"Not this time," I said.

This was not good. I was trying not to panic, but I knew the likelihood of the car miraculously starting or me getting us a ride and tow out of there was very low. Tow trucks weren't easy to come by this far out, and with the weather the way it was we would be lucky to get someone to come get it at all. With it being Christmas Eve night, it was even harder to get someone to come out.

Still, I had to try. Otherwise we were going to be stuck there until morning, and I didn't know if two blankets was going to be enough. I pulled open my phone again, glad I had charged it all the way on the car charger before I shut the car off, and dialed the number for the only tow guy in town.

It was busy. I tried again and got the busy signal once more. Holly was focused on her crocheting and I waited a little bit, hoping to get through and at least leave a message. The clock on my phone flipped, signifying five full minutes since the last call. I hit the call button again.

"Munton's Towing," a voice said on the other end of the line, and I exhaled loudly. I was positive I was going to get a voicemail.

"Oh, thank goodness," I said. "I know it's Christmas Eve, but I'm stuck on the side of the road on 18. Right at the mile marker 13, actually. The snow got so bad I had to pull off and shut off the engine, and now it won't get going. Is there any way you could come pick us up?"

"You're on 18?" he asked "Marker 13? Where are you headed?"

"Back to the east side of town," I said. "The old mansion up there off of Carter's Road."

"Yeah, I know that place," the driver said. "Good news is that's right by where I am. Bad news is getting on 18 right now isn't a good idea. The plows haven't been able to hit it yet, and it's a disaster out there."

"Trust me, I know," I said. "I'm stuck in it."

"Well, dang," the man on the other end, who I assumed was the Munton of Munton's Towing, said.

"If you could help us out, I would greatly appreciate it. I can pay you in cash tonight if you can pick us up."

"It's not the money, sir, though I appreciate the offer," he said. "It's just the danger of the situation. It's Christmas Eve, and all my other drivers are either already out or went home. I'd have to come get you myself, and that's a good little ways out there."

"I understand," I said. "But we would really appreciate the effort."

There was silence on the other end for a moment while I let the man think about the situation. He cleared his throat and seemed to make a sipping sound, like he was drinking something. Suddenly, I wanted a hot cocoa more than anything else in the entire world. Warm, happy visions of sitting by the fire with Holly and sipping one filled my head.

"All right, I'll tell you what," he said. "I'll come get you myself. But it might be a little while, so just hang in there. Are you somewhere safe?"

"Off to the side of the road," I said. "But no one else is out here, so I think we're okay."

"Do you have blankets or anything to keep you warm?" he asked.

I looked over at Holly. I couldn't tell for sure, but it seemed like there was the tiniest hint of a smirk on her lips.

"Yes," I said. "We have two blankets, but they aren't very thick."

"Good. It won't be that long. I'll get you home for Christmas. Just hang in there," he said.

I thanked him and he hung up the phone. Sitting back in the seat, I pulled the blanket up over my shoulders and sighed. What kind of mess had I gotten us into? I opened my big, fat mouth and said something I shouldn't have, and now I was stuck in the car with her, having put us both in danger and getting stuck in the snow.

"All we can do is wait," Holly said. "Good news is, if we're here long enough I will have made a third blanket we can use."

I tried to laugh, but couldn't. I was too worried. She was right, all we could do was wait. But all I could think about was the hope that Christmas wouldn't be ruined.

Chapter Sixty-Seven

Lawson

Hours later the car had grown cold, and what little hope I had of getting back to the house before midnight was dwindling. The snow was still coming down, but not as heavy. The car was stuck though, and nothing I could do would get it going again. We had to stay where we were, in the car, bundled up in what blankets we had, until the tow truck could get to us.

I checked the clock on the phone. Eleven-fifteen. We'd been in the car for over two hours now. It was getting really cold. I swiped it open and called the tow driver again.

"Munton's," the voice answered on the other end.

"Hey, just checking in on if you have an ETA," I said.

"Not yet," he said. "There's nothing I can do really. All my drivers are out, and I had to go get one of them because they were stuck before I could come to you. I'm on my way now, but I have to tell you, it's rough out there. It will take me a bit. I'm doing the best I can, though."

"I know, and I appreciate it," I said. "It's just cold."

"I understand," he said. "I hate that you guys are stuck out there, but I can't move any faster than I am. I'll let you know when I'm close."

"Thank you," I said, and hung up.

"I don't think I can crochet anymore. My fingers are numb," Holly said. "Plus, even with the snow, it's dark."

"It is," I said. "Come here."

I flipped the console over so that the space between us was empty and we both scooted a little closer to each other. I didn't realize just how cold the seats were until I moved. Leaving the place where my backside had made it warmer to a cooler spot was alarming, but the reward was worth it. Holly curled into my arms and we wrapped both blankets around us on top of each other, effectively trapping the heat better.

Holly's head rested on my chest as we sat in the quiet. The snow had piled high on the windshield and every so often I would turn the battery on to use the wiper, but it was immediately covered again only seconds later. Thankfully the driver's window was facing away from the wind and stayed relatively clear, though it fogged up easily. If the headlights of the tow truck were coming, it would be the only way I would see them.

I checked my phone again. Eleven-twenty. The weather app showed that it was ten degrees.

It was almost Christmas. For all the preparation we did, for all the building up of the day I had made to her and in my own head, this was how we were going to ring in the holiday. Stuck on the side of the road, freezing, and hoping that we could get picked up before we both had icicles dripping from our noses.

"You know," Holly said, "this reminds me of something."

"This?" I asked. "Being trapped in a snowstorm in a car?"

She nodded, her breath warm on my chest.

"I was about six, I think. I was staying with my other grandmother while on Christmas break, right before Christmas. It was a weird time with my parents. They were trying to work things out. So, I spent a few days here and there with my grandma, which I didn't mind because she just let me do whatever. If I wanted to stay up late and watch '50s TV show reruns, I could.

"Anyway, she had this tiny little house. No more than a thousand square feet. Two bedrooms, both the size of matchboxes. She didn't have central heat in the house but there was this big fireplace in the center, and when it was going it kept the whole place warm.

"Then, one day, Granny asked if I wanted to go to the store with her. I was excited because that meant she was going to get something specific to make. She didn't just go to the store. It was always a set day, so if she was randomly going on a different day it meant she was up to something."

"My mom was like that. She grocery shopped on Monday. Only Monday."

"Right," Holly said, "like that. She was nearly religious about it. So, I figured, hey, I'm getting cookies or something out of this deal, and hopped into the car. The snow had already hit us, but it was snowing again when we went out. Just light stuff. Then we got back to the car from inside the store and it was coming down really hard. Granny tried to comfort me, but I was afraid.

"We started down the road, and Granny hit a patch of ice and skidded off through a guardrail. Thankfully, it was just one of those ones they set up way before a bridge and we didn't go anywhere except this grassy median. But we were stuck there. The snow was heavy and we ended up waiting until this guy in a pickup saw us and helped push it out. I remember yanking on the steering wheel while they pushed, trying to help get it out."

"Wow," I said. "That's crazy."

She nodded, snuggling harder into my chest.

"When we got back, my Gran was so happy she made a bunch of cookies and ended up calling the man who helped us out of the ditch. He swung by and picked up a dozen of them to take home to his family. I'll never forget how jealous I was he was getting my cookies, but Gran made sure I had plenty."

"Good grandma," I said.

"The best. I had two amazing grandmas," she said. "What about you? Have you ever been trapped in a car in the snow before?"

"Sure, loads of times," I said. "But usually in the middle of a city and not on an isolated, dark road. I drive a lot for my work, though, and going through places like Chicago and Minneapolis, snow is a common thing. I've had to pull over and wait out storms before."

"I bet," she said.

I wondered if she was bristling at the mention of my life away from Snowflake Hollow. A life that seemed so far away right now. But still, my life. Where did Holly fit into that? It was a question we were both going to have to address soon. But not now. Not while we depended on each other's body heat for warmth. Not while we had our Christmas wish distilled simply to being back at the house, cozied up by the fire.

"Better thoughts," I said. "Let's focus on better thoughts. What's your favorite Christmas memory?"

"Oh, you *would* ask me that," she said. "Does this year count?"

"No."

"Why?" she asked. "That was my best Christmas memory, hands down."

"Nope, something from childhood. Go."

"All right," she said. "Let me think about it. You first."

I laughed and shook my head.

"Mine is easy," I said. "The Christmas after I turned eight."

"What happened?" she asked.

"Well, we were living in the house I grew up in, right? It was on this little street with a couple of neighborhood kids I played with all the time. Good house, good memories. But Christmas was especially fun because we would all decorate the house like crazy."

"I figured you had," she said. "You seem to be an expert at it."

I shrugged.

"I got good at it. Especially later on when I was a teenager. I used to sell my services to my neighbors, going around with a ladder and offering to help them put up lights. I wanted to make a business out of it when I grew up, but I quickly realized there wasn't much of a market for it outside of old folks," I said.

"And me," Holly said. "But carry on."

I laughed.

"True. Anyway, I was eight, and I was starting to figure out we didn't have much money, you know? So, when I filled out my Christmas list, I intentionally didn't put anything too expensive. I didn't know how it worked, but I had a feeling that my mom read my letter to Santa and tried to get what she could. So I made a second, secret letter to send to him with all the expensive stuff on it."

"Like the kids at the Children's Hospital," Holly said.

"Sort of," I said. "Anyway, I made this second letter and got a stamp on my way home from school and everything. I put it in the mailbox without telling Mom and then sat back to enjoy Christmas. It was only a day or two before Christmas Eve when I did that, but hey, Santa is magic, right?

"So, Christmas morning comes and there are a bunch of gifts under the tree, but I didn't see the one that was on top of the list for Santa."

"What was it?"

"A bike, specifically this Huffy bike I'd had my eye on at the sporting goods store for months. It was expensive, or at least relatively expensive, and when I didn't see it I was a little crushed. I tried not to show it, but I was. Then Mom asked if something was wrong and I said there was just something I had asked Santa for that I didn't get, but that it was okay since I got so many great things.

"I'll never forget, she just took a sip of her coffee and smiled and looked at me and said, 'Maybe you should look out the window.'"

"No way," Holly said.

"Yup. I glanced out the window and sure enough, that bike was sitting in the driveway with a big red bow on it. I exploded I was so happy. I ran outside in my pajamas and jumped onto it and took off down the cul-de-sac. Mom stood on the porch and laughed, sipping her coffee and watching me for a little bit before calling me back in. When I got there, she had tears in her eyes and I asked her why and she just shook her head saying she was happy.

"Come to find out years later, she had noticed me salivating over that bike in the summer and saved for months to buy it for me. She got it the weekend before Christmas and it was the last one left. She had been so nervous she would miss it, she said she cried herself to sleep a couple nights. She just wanted to give me a good Christmas, and boy, she nailed it."

"That's an amazing story," Holly said. "Your mom is a wonderful woman."

"She is," I said, a pang of sadness gripping my heart. It was lessened this time because of Holly's head resting above it, though. Just a little bit less sharp. "She truly is."

"I don't want to miss Christmas morning," Holly said after a few seconds. Her voice was low and sad and my heart broke for her. If I thought I could make it without us both dying of exposure I would have offered to carry her on my back all the way there right then. But that would be crazy. Wouldn't it? "Not for that little boy. He's counting on us."

"I know," I said, pulling her tight and glancing at my phone. Eleven-forty. "I know. We won't, though. We are not going to miss Christmas morning. I promise."

Chapter Sixty-Eight

Holly

"What are you doing?" I asked as Lawson shifted in the seat and moved out from behind me. He wrapped the blanket around me tightly and then put his hand on the handle of the driver's door.

"Don't go anywhere," he said. "When I open this door it's going to let out a lot of heat, so I'm going to go as fast as I can. Just stay here."

"What?" I asked, shocked. "You can't go out there. It's freezing!"

"I'm not walking all the way back," he said. "Just to the nearest exit. It should be for Gayton Road. There's a Sheetz up there that's twenty-four-hours. I just need to make it there and find someone to help us. It's almost Christmas, and we are going to be home for it."

I was about to respond when what he said hit me like a ton of bricks. He called it home. My heart warmed and my cheeks blushed in spite of the cold.

"You can't go without me," I said. "Either we both stay or we both go."

Lawson's eyes narrowed and he paused for a few moments before finally nodding.

"Okay," he said. "But bring the blankets. Wrap them around you."

"You take one of them," I said. "You need to stay warm, too."

"I'll be fine," he said. "You need to keep warm."

I realized he wasn't going to take any other arguments from that as he turned his attention out the window. Then, grabbing a duffel bag from the back, he opened it up and started rummaging through it. He pulled out a couple of older looking t-shirts, a couple pairs of white socks, and a pack of gum.

"First, how much stuff do you have in there, and second, why the gum?"

"I always have a gym bag with a couple pairs of clothes to change in to," he said. "I told you, I travel a lot and sometimes I don't have the chance to go home and get clothes to change in to. The gum will help keep you warm." He must have seen the expression on my face change pretty dramatically. "It's true. Chomping on gum while you're cold will actually trick your brain into thinking it's warmer. Take one."

Shrugging, I grabbed a stick and put it in my mouth. It was seasonally minty and I reached down to grabbed the bag with the gift we had fought so hard to get. The crocheting could stay in the nice dry car, but that toy was coming with us.

"So what's with the socks and stuff?" I asked as he stuffed them down in his coat pocket and zipped the pocket closed.

"We both have snow boots on," he said, "but snow is going to come down into the boots. When we get somewhere warm, we need to change into the new socks to keep ourselves warmer. Same with the shirts, though we might not need them as badly as the socks."

"Smart," I said. "There is nothing in the world I hate more than cold, wet socks."

"Seconded," he said. "All right, are you ready?"

I glanced behind him, out the driver's door at the landscape I could see. It was cold and dark, and the snow was piled high on the ground. It was going to be difficult to walk through, much less try to walk for a couple of miles if needed. I wasn't sure where the next exit was. All I knew was that if I was going to make it, I was going to make it because I was standing side by side with Lawson. If he was there with me, I felt like I could do it.

"Ready," I said.

"Here we go," he said. "Come out my side, behind me."

He opened the door, and a rush of cold air almost made me want to give up before I even started. It was the biting kind of cold air, the kind that got down into your lungs. The minty gum probably didn't help, and I shuddered. Lawson was out of the car and I had to move, though, so I scooted out, trying to keep the blankets wrapped around me from falling down into the snow.

"Adventure," I muttered as my feet sank into the snow. Thank goodness I had worn the ones with the fur lining. So far my feet hadn't gotten cold, and hopefully would stay that way for a little while. The rest of my wasn't as lucky, despite how warmly I had dressed.

Lawson started heading around the car, going in the direction we had been driving. I caught up to him and looked behind us. The place where we pulled off the road was invisible already, having been covered by new snow. Pretty soon the whole car would be buried in it.

"How far back was the last exit before here?" I asked.

"A couple of miles," he said. "That's why I was going this way toward Gayton. I'm pretty sure it's only about a mile or two away."

"Only," I said mostly to myself, but it got a laugh from him.

"I know, I don't want to be doing it either," he said. "But just think of how nice it's going to be to have a nice warm cup of cocoa and sit by the fire once we get back."

"That does sound nice," I said. "We could just bring blankets down and sleep on the floor and wait for the guests to get up."

"Don't tempt me," he said, laughing. "No, I think I'll want a mattress under my back after all this."

"Good point," I said. "With big, fluffy, warm socks."

"Yes," he said. "I might have to borrow some of yours."

"Gladly," I said. "Pink or purple?"

"I am secure enough in my manhood to accept either," he said, grinning, "but there was also a green pair I saw the other day."

"In the wash," I said. "Though freshly dried fluffy socks sounds like a dream right now."

"That it does," he said.

We tried to keep talking as we trudged on, wanting to distract ourselves from the mission at hand. I felt like we must have gone over a mile, but there was no sign in sight. Finally, I decided to just keep my head down and focus on the path I was making in the snow rather than looking for the exit. It would come when it came.

Lawson was in the middle of saying something about a recipe he had seen on a baking show recently when he stopped cold and I looked up to him. He was smiling hard.

"There it is," he said, pointing. "Gayton Road exit!"

Laughing, we both took off, the exhaustion in our bones fading a little as we ran toward the sign. When we reached it, we peered down a ways and Lawson whistled under his breath.

"What?" I asked.

"Just noticing what the other sign says. The Sheetz is a half-mile off the ramp. We have a bit more walking to do," he said.

"Okay, that might be," I said, trying to keep our spirits up, "but we can do it. It's not that far. Let's go."

"Holly White, queen of positivity," he chuckled.

"Hey, that's your fault," I said. "I was content to be a grump. You're the one who turned me into a cheerful Christmas person."

"Guilty," he said. "All right, let's go."

That last half mile was a doozy. We could see the Sheetz in the distance almost immediately, but it felt like it took forever to get there. By the time we did, my legs were sore and my lungs hurt from breathing in so much cold air. And just like Lawson thought, my socks were wet. Not a lot, but enough. The effect was making me even colder.

We finally got to the door and opened it up. A blast of warm air hit us and we stood in the doorway, our eyes closed as we let the air hit us for a moment. When the hot air stopped blowing, we opened our eyes to see a very confused and concerned clerk behind the counter.

"Can I help you?" he asked meekly.

"Our car broke down," Lawson said. "We need a ride home."

"Oh, that's terrible," he said. "Unfortunately, I'm the only person working here tonight. I can't close the place down and leave."

Lawson hung his head and nodded.

"I understand. Do you mind if we hang out here and warm up, maybe ask anyone that comes by if we can get a ride?"

"That's fine," he said. "Are you hungry? We have some hot French fries. My treat."

"Those do sound good," I said.

"Of course. Merry Christmas," the clerk said, beaming.

He made a basket of the fries and we sat down in one of the booths by the windows. I made the dash to the bathroom first, changing socks and coming back out feeling a good bit better. Lawson was next, and when he came out he joined me to eat fries and chat with the clerk.

Only a few minutes into our impromptu midnight snack, a red truck pulled in to the station. It had a large snowplow on the front of it. Lawson jumped to his feet and I hopped up to follow him. A little old man who looked rather familiar was going to the pump, and when he saw Lawson he smiled a bright, cheery smile that was completely disarming. His long white beard rose with his cheeks, which were red and merry.

"Hello," he said as we approached. "Merry Christmas."

"Merry Christmas," Lawson said. "I hate to bother you, but you aren't by chance heading toward Snowflake Hollow, are you?"

"I am actually," he said. "I was taking my plow down 18 to clear a bit of road and head over to Roanoke after."

I recognized Roanoke as the town a dozen or so miles south of where we were, and my eyes lit up. I looked at Lawson, who looked just as excited as I was.

"Our car broke down on 18," I said. "We actually walked here from where our car is parked. It won't start and a tow truck is on the way to get it, but it could be a while. We really don't want to miss Christmas at home. Do you think you could drive us to Snowflake Hollow?"

He didn't even flinch.

"Of course I can," he said. "My name's Nick. What's yours?"

"Oh thank you, Nick." Lawson said, and I wondered if he made the same connection I did. "My name is Lawson Lane, and this is Holly White."

"Nice to meet you two," he said. "Hop on in the truck. I'll get you there in no time at all."

"Thank you so much," I said. "I could just hug you."

"Well, by all means," he laughed, and held out his arms. I took him up on it and squeezed him tight. He smelled like candy canes.

We went back inside to say goodnight to the clerk and thank him for his hospitality, and while we were there Lawson paid for Nick's gas. When we went out again, Nick thanked him for that and laughed a laugh that was so booming, so cheerful, that I felt tears form in the corners of my eyes. We were experiencing a real, live Christmas miracle.

The drive back was quicker than I expected it to be, and Nick played a variety of Christmas songs on the way down. I couldn't help but sing along as we made our way into Snowflake Hollow and to the bed and breakfast. When he dropped us off, he waved out of the window and we waved back.

"Merry Christmas," he said as he drove away. "Goodnight!"

"Did he..." Lawson asked. "Was he..."

"Come on," I said grinning. "I have some fluffy socks with your name on them in there."

Chapter Sixty-Nine

Lawson

I opened the door as quietly as possible, not wanting to disturb anyone who was already asleep or alert anyone who might have dozed off by the fire. Thankfully the main room was empty, and the guests had done a good job of cleaning up after themselves for once. The dishwasher was even running.

I smiled. I was starting to think like Holly about the place. My first thoughts were how I could get the place in order and take some of the burden off of her.

Holly followed me in and immediately took up residence in front of the fire. I smiled and headed into the kitchen. It wasn't like I didn't want to be in front of the fire, too, but I wanted to take care of her more. She laid the blankets down on the hearth and peeled off her socks, warming her toes by the fire while I got some mugs out of the cabinet and poured some cocoa and a purely childish number of marshmallows into them. Eggnog would come later, but for now it was time to warm ourselves up.

As I handed Holly her mug, she looked up at me and I felt my heart tug again. She was so beautiful. I sat down beside her and warmed myself by the fire as I took a deep sip of the cocoa. It was probably too hot to drink, but I didn't care. I drank it anyway.

We sat in the quiet for a while, drinking our drinks until the ice seemed to melt from our bones. Eventually Holly reached over and grabbed the remote control, turning on a Christmas music station, and smiled at me. I shook my head and smiled back.

"Time to get some stuff wrapped," she said. "Ready for a long night?"

"If it's with you, doing this, absolutely."

She smiled and ventured off to her room where the gifts had been hidden. Meanwhile, I went to the closet in the pantry where the wrapping paper was kept since it was brought in from the garage, and set up a little wrapping station. Then I dipped into the kitchen to make some rum-free eggnog.

Strictly speaking, eggnog without the rum wasn't really eggnog as far as I was concerned. But we both were already exhausted and had a lot of wrapping to do before the guests woke up, so staying alert was a top priority. Therefore the rum had to stay in the bottle.

I flipped on a couple of lamps, giving the room some more light, and joined Holly on the floor, sitting cross-legged and grabbing my assigned pair of scissors.

"Shall we begin?" I asked, getting a laugh from Holly.

"We shall," she said. "But first, I wanted to show you something."

"What's that?"

The bag that had held the toy we went out to get also had another bag inside. As she pulled it out, I recognized it as the crocheting she was doing in the car, which I thought she had left in it.

"What?" I asked. "You brought it!"

"I did," she said. "I didn't think I did, but it must have fallen in while I was scooting out of the car. I'm glad it did, though. I'll have it finished in about five minutes and then it will be ready to give away."

"What is it, exactly?" I asked. "All I can see is that really pretty pattern."

"It's a blanket," she said, unfolding it and spreading it out for my first time seeing it. "I made a bunch of them. I was going to give them to the Children's Hospital so they can give them to the kids as a special gift from Mrs. Claus. What do you think?"

"I think it's beautiful," I said. "And I think you are incredible."

I leaned over our wrapping station and planted a soft kiss on her lips.

"Good," she said. "Because I'm going to do this while you get to wrapping stuff, then I'll make the gift basket and join you on the wrapping."

"I just want you to know that I wrap gifts like an idiot," I said. "I never quite got the hang of it."

"I can help," Holly sighed. "Show me what you do."

Within minutes Holly was crouched over me, showing me where to fold, where to cut, and where to tape. I knew she suspected I was doing it on purpose, but it didn't stop her. I was glad, too, since I absolutely was.

After I started to get the hang of it, Holly went back to doing her gift baskets. We chatted a little, mostly continuing our conversation from before about good Christmas memories, of which for her there weren't many. I took the lead on making sure the conversation stayed lighter, and regaled her with various stories of our family Christmases.

Each present was tucked under the tree with great care. And when we finally got to the last one, the toy that had sparked our crazy journey, Holly put a big red bow on it and placed it right in front.

"You know," I said, "these cookies have to be eaten before the guests wake up in the morning."

"Uh-huh," Holly said. "Those are supposed to be for Santa."

"Well, see, here's the thing," I said. "Santa is on a diet. I, however, am not."

"Well, if we're just looking out for Santa's diet," Holly said, laughing and reaching over to take one of the cookies. "I suppose it's okay."

Sitting on the couch, facing the tree and the fire, we sat down and dug into the cookies. The sun was going to be rising soon, and we didn't have a whole lot of time before things got crazy around there. But sitting there with Holly, watching the fire and eating milk and cookies, was as good a way to spend a little bit of time as any.

"I can't imagine spending Christmas morning at a bed and breakfast," I said, staring at the toy that caused so much grief, wrapped in some jaunty wrapping paper with its giant bow. "Nothing against this place, but it would be so weird not to be at home."

"I guess," Holly said. "He seems to be having a good time, though. He's got his family with him."

"That's probably all that matters," I said, nodding. "Wherever his parents are, that's home. It's just a big deal not to be home when Christmas comes."

"You're not home," she said. "And you seem to be all right."

I pulled her tighter and kissed the top of her head.

"True," I said. "I feel pretty good being here on Christmas."

"Sun is coming up," Holly said, gesturing to the window. "I have a feeling we're going to have guests up and about in a couple of hours at the latest. We should get some sleep."

"A nap sounds good," I said. "And then a second nap later sounds even better."

Holly laughed, maneuvering herself up and off the couch and holding out a hand to me. I took it and stood, letting her lead me upstairs. We went into her room, shut the door, and stripped down to just our underwear before crawling into the bed. It was still cold in the house, even with the heat on, but nothing could be as cold as we were in the car. Comparatively, we were very warm.

I laid back in the bed and Holly curled up in the crook of my shoulder, resting her head on my chest and draping one arm over me. I held her there, letting one hand drape over her shoulder, and kissed the top of her head. Within minutes, we were both happily and deeply asleep.

Chapter Seventy

Holly

This was what everything had been building toward. The big day. The day of The Claus. Christmas.

So many days building up to this day, so many events and shopping days and late night discussions about how to make this day as special as possible, and now it was here. I just had to execute.

I shifted nervously on my feet in front of the oven. Should I open the door? If I did, would it let the heat out and ruin everything? Or should I wait until the timer went off and hope? I knew what Lawson would say. 'Trust the recipe'. But I had done that before and ended up with top pie crusts that were better served as throwing discs.

Just thirty more seconds and then I could open it up. The shifting was getting faster. I was going from toes to toes rather than heel to heel. I shook my hands at the wrist and took a long, deep breath. The timer went off and my fingers were already pulling on the oven door.

No billow of smoke. That was a good sign.

No awful smell. Two for two.

I opened the door all the way and peered inside, the heat of the oven washing over my face.

No briquettes on the tray. Just perfectly fluffy, amazing-looking cinnamon rolls.

Three for three.

I stifled a little cheer and grabbed the oven mitt to pull the sheet out. Setting it down on the burners, I beamed down at my creations. I did it.

Perfect cinnamon rolls to serve for Christmas morning breakfast. And they smelled *so good*. I didn't have to light a candle or stand in front of the window or anything. This was fantastic.

Immediately, I grabbed another batch and stuck them in the oven, setting the timer and closing the door. I knew I needed to do it right then, or else I was going to be so distracted by my success I would forget.

Grabbing the rolls, I brought them over to the table and peeled them off the tray and onto a serving plate. They didn't stick and tear, which was another miracle. As soon as they were on the plate, I grabbed my icing materials. I wanted to do it while they were still hot. That way they got extra gooey.

Like all the baking shows Lawson and I had watched together, the icing went on and started to drip between the folds. I was having to keep myself from drooling as I finished them, and was contemplating ripping off a few of them to test. My fingers were on two of them, prepared to pull them apart, when Lawson came in.

Kissing me on my cheek, he went around me and stared down at the magical creations on the table and whistled low.

"Merry Christmas," he said, still looking down at the rolls. "These look amazing. You finally did it. You made Christmas morning cinnamon rolls."

He opened his arms to me and I curled into his chest.

"They're from a can," I admitted. "Brenda isn't open today, and Giuseppe doesn't make cinnamon rolls. You would think he would since he's the bread guy and all, but there it is."

Lawson laughed and pulled me tight.

"I don't care," he said. "You baked them. Good enough for me." Our noses brushed and he pressed a soft kiss to my lips. When he spoke again it was barely above a whisper. "Are you ready for Christmas celebration?"

I nodded, but it was partially a lie. What I was really ready for was pulling him upstairs and just spending the rest of the day with him, feeding each other cinnamon rolls and lying around in bed. But there were duties left, and we had to fulfill them.

We sat at the table and ate our cinnamon rolls in the quiet, relishing the last few minutes before the chaos of Christmas morning. With the lights twinkling on the tree and the presents overflowing around it, the fire burning bright and cinnamon rolls to eat, it was nearly perfect. Once we were done with breakfast Lawson took our plates away, leaving the rest of the rolls on the serving tray, and I went into the living room.

On the floor above, I could hear the sound of little footsteps joined quickly by bigger, heavier ones. The guests were getting up, and it would only be seconds before it all began. I looked back at Lawson as he came into the room and the smile on his face was infectious. He loved this. I was starting to feel like I might love it, too.

Lawson flipped the lights off, leaving only the lamps and the light of the tree, giving the room a glow, just as the little boy came barreling down the steps. He made a beeline for the tree, diving to his knees in a way that made my own knees ache a little. He reached for the present with the big bow and held it up to show his parents, who had made it into the room.

Vicky was a little bleary-eyed, and I noticed her shake her head slightly.

"Does it have your name on it?" she asked. "Look at the tag. Only get the ones with your name on them."

Vint looked at the tag again and nodded. "It does. It has my name on it."

Vicky looked over at Gary, who gave her a hint of a shrug. Neither one of them could confirm to the other that they had wrapped that gift and put it under the tree, because neither one of them had. But they didn't want to make a show of it and call Vint's attention. So when Gary came and sat down beside his wife, offering her a cinnamon roll, they put on slightly confused fake smiles and watched their son.

Lawson joined me, handing me a cup of coffee and taking my hand.

Vint took the gift and brought it over to his mother, setting it down beside her and running back to the tree. Next, he grabbed his mother's stocking, then his father's, and brought them over. They looked at their little boy curiously as he stood there watching them.

"Honey, you can open your gifts," Vicky said.

"But it's your Christmas, too, Mommy. We should open stockings together."

My heart squeezed, and I felt Lawson reposition himself on the couch. He was trying to hide his emotion, too. I leaned my head on his shoulder as the mother and father began digging things out of the stockings which I had packed so tightly that I couldn't even fit another candy cane in them.

As they opened their stockings, the other couple staying at the inn came down. Jeremy headed for the tree to get the present he'd left there for Daisy, but his eyes caught the stockings waiting for them. They widened and he looked up at me, glanced at Vint, then back to me.

"Santa brought us stockings, too?" he asked.

I nodded.

"He said *everyone* should have a Merry Christmas," Lawson said.

The man mouthed 'thank you' and sat down next to his wife with a wide grin. We watched them dig through and find all the fun treats and surprises I had snuck in there. Even Vint's stocking had a few extras that Santa had dropped by stuffed in along with what his parents had given me when I told them I was filling a stocking for him. They didn't know the adults were getting goodies as well, and it was fun watching them rediscover the joy of those childhood Christmas mornings discovering silly toys, candy, and other treats in their own stockings.

When the stockings were finally gone through and candy was already being consumed, it was time for the presents.

The one with the red bow stayed next to Vicky while the other gifts were doled out. I could tell that she and Gary were feeling nervous about the opening. Vint was already happy and excited, but both looked a little anxious, like they just knew their son was about to be disappointed. I wanted to go over and reassure them, but I couldn't figure out a way to do it without spoiling the surprise for the little boy. I'd just have to be patient. It wouldn't be long before he opened it, and they would get the thrill of the surprise as well.

At one point, as the gifts were being opened, I got up and went into the kitchen, fetching a new cup of eggnog and grabbing another cinnamon roll. As I went into the room again, Lawson was watching me and I shrugged, taking a bite of the roll. He laughed and shook his head.

"What?" I asked as I sat back down beside him. "Christmas calories don't count."

"Then I'm going to get another one, too," he said.

"Do it," I teased, trying to fit a foot of roll into my mouth at once. He eyed my eggnog. "It doesn't have any alcohol. I'm trying to learn to be a purist."

Lawson laughed as he hopped up and went into the kitchen, grabbing his own roll and a new mug of coffee. Sitting down beside me, we curled up together, pigging out while watching the festivities. It was like a snapshot of something more, something perhaps in our future. But I didn't want to think about that. I just wanted to enjoy the moment.

"No way!!" Vint said, squealing. I knew what that meant. He had opened the box with the red bow.

"What is it, buddy?" his dad asked.

"It's the Johnny Omega, Kenny Moxley double pack! With the limited edition accessories!" he shouted. "Santa found it! He found my two favorite wrestlers!"

Gary looked at his wife, who had the same stunned expression as him. They looked over at us. His eyes were wide and tears formed at the corners as we both held up our hands, like we were completely innocent, shrugging to show we had no idea how that showed up under the tree. A smile spread across his lips and he dove into a world of play with his son. They ripped open the package and began wrestling the toys together, squeals of delight coming from them both.

"See?" the little boy said as he held up his toy. "Magic!"

That was all it took for me to tear up completely. I was surprised by it. I thought I had more control of myself than that, that all this Christmas hubbub, while I was feeling it, wasn't that strong. That I was playing along in a way.

Not now. Now I knew it was real. I pressed my face into Lawson's arms and let his shirt sleeve soak up my tears.

Chapter Seventy-One

Lawson

Holly was starting to get very emotional, and I could see it could become something she would be upset at herself over later. She wouldn't want to break down in front of her guests. She wanted so badly to look like this was effortless for her, just a part of being the world's best bed and breakfast owner. Only, I knew better. I knew how hard she worked, how much she worried over making sure everything was perfect.

I squeezed her hand and she lifted her face to look into mine. A thick strand of hair running away from the ponytail she had pulled back in rebellion stuck to her cheek with a tear. I wiped the wetness away and brushed the hair back over her ear.

"Hey, come with me," I said.

"Where?"

"The tree, silly," I said.

I pulled her to her feet, and we walked across the room. Looking back at the families enjoying their gifts and chatting with each other, she smiled, and I kissed her head. She deserved to see how things came together after how hard she'd worked.

"I got you a little something," I said.

I reached down and pulled up the biggest present left under the tree, the one I was most excited for. She unwrapped it quickly, tearing at the paper and tossing it aside. The logo was revealed almost immediately, ruining any tension almost instantaneously. But I didn't care. The look on her face was worth it anyway.

"You bought me a new coffeemaker?" she asked, a combination of laughter and that touched 'aww' sound people make coming out of her afterward.

I nodded.

"I did," I said, proudly. "You have no idea how hard it was not to give it to you before now."

"Oh, I bet," she said, giggling. "Poor boy, you've had to suffer with sub-par coffee for so long."

"Look," I said, ignoring the teasing, "it has all kinds of little settings. You can make a whole pot or make individual cups, and set the temperature and everything. It even has a little compartment for sugar and creamers."

"It's wonderful," she said, holding it to her chest. "Now your turn."

Holly bent over and reached under the tree, pulling out a perfectly wrapped gift that I didn't remember seeing her wrap. She was a sneaky one when she wanted to be. I ripped open the packaging and my jaw dropped. It was a blanket, made in dark coffee colors, that she had made for me.

"You made this for me?" I asked. "I saw you working on this!"

"I did," she said, smiling wide. "I call it the coffee blanket. What do you think?"

"I think it's amazing," I said. "Thank you so much."

I pulled her in for a hug and noticed that there was something hard inside the blanket. Pulling back, I unwrapped it carefully and found what she had hidden inside. A bottle of the local moonshiner's top shelf rum and some cookie cutters. It was so thoughtful, so personal and sweet that I pulled her in again, hugging her tight to my chest and kissing her head.

"Thank you," I said. "This... this means a lot to me."

"I'm glad," she said, obviously pleased with herself. "Now, do you think we can get the guests in to eat breakfast? I noticed a couple already snagged rolls, but I think we need to get the rest eating before they forget."

"I think we can convince them if we tell them that it's cinnamon rolls, yes," I said, laughing.

"Hey, everybody," Holly said, taking a step toward them and raising her voice just enough to be heard over the laughter and chatting. "I have fresh baked cinnamon rolls in the dining room, along with coffee and orange juice and some eggnog for anyone that wants some."

"All right!" Vint said. "I want some cinnamon rolls, Daddy!"

"Then let's get some," his father said, taking him by the hand.

Slowly, the entire group of guests made their way into the dining room and started digging in. I hooked up the new coffee maker and made us both inaugural cups from it, and we bundled up to step outside and get a breath of fresh air.

We didn't plan to be outside long, but it was nice to get away from the inside for just a second. I had longed just to be inside all evening last evening, to get away from the cold and the wet. But that was after a long day and with a ton of stress on my shoulders. Now, even though I didn't sleep a lot, I had some, and the big part of the day was over.

We stood silently, sipping our coffee as we leaned into each other and looked out over the fallen snow. It glittered like diamonds in the sunshine.

"This is really good," Holly said. "What flavor did you say this one was?"

"Maple macchiato," I said. "The box came with a few pods, and I thought I would try them out first. The old machine you have was confounding and terrible."

"It is," she admitted. "But this is spectacular. Here's to good coffee."

We clinked our mugs together and sipped again.

"All in all," she said, "I think this was a very successful Christmas."

"Me, too."

As the words escaped my lips, a tow truck pulled around the corner. My face fell, and then slowly a laugh built up inside me. What timing.

"That's my car."

The laugh became full and loud, and Holly joined me.

I was still laughing when she returned from dipping inside, coming back with a paper napkin full of cookies and a Styrofoam cup full of hot cocoa. She handed them to me and I brought them down to the driver, Munton, and we spoke for a minute at the edge of the drive. Then he dropped the car off and waved the cookies out the window at Holly.

"These are delicious," he called out. "Thank you! Merry Christmas!"

"Merry Christmas!" she called out to him.

"That was a very Snowflake Hollow thing to do, you know," I said as I made it back to her.

"What, the cookies?" she asked.

"And the cocoa," I said. "Maybe this place is in your heart after all."

"Maybe it is," she said, placing her forehead against mine and closing her eyes for a moment. "Maybe it is."

A little while and a small nap later, we got dressed and went over to see Mom. The shawls and blankets Holly made for the folks at the center were ready in the bag, and when we got inside she started handing them out. The folks there loved them, and when we got to Mom she was thrilled to see us and gave us both a big hug.

We sat with them for a little while, talking and chatting and noticed that there were a couple of people there who didn't seem to have any family with them. Holly mentioned it to me, and I mentioned them to Mom.

"Are they alone?" I asked.

"Oh, yes, that's Gerard and Samantha. Gerard's children couldn't make it this year. Samantha doesn't have any, and her sister passed away a few months ago," she said.

"So they don't have anyone?" I asked.

Sadly, she shook her head no.

"Well, I have an idea," Holly said. "Why don't you come over to the bed and breakfast for Christmas dinner. Invite them to come with us. We can have a celebration there and they won't be left alone for the holiday."

"Are you sure?" Mom asked. "That would be absolutely wonderful."

"Sure," Holly said. "Come on. Let's get you packed up."

She smiled and went over to the two of them while Holly and I packed up her things. Holly said she wanted to make sure that she had enough there that, if she needed to, she could stay the night in one of the empty rooms. I packed everything she would need, and we put it in the car before coming back. The two people she spoke to were smiling wide, and the gentleman flicked a tear from the corner of his eye.

"Hello," he said as we joined them again. "My name is Gerard. Your mother says that you would like us to join you for Christmas dinner?"

"Yup," I said, shaking his hand. "I'm Lawson. This is Holly. We'd like you folks to come over if you don't have anything else pressing."

"I don't," Samantha said. "I'd love to come."

"Will there be cookies?" Gerard asked slyly.

"A mountain of them," I said.

Gerard smacked his hands together and smiled.

"Hot dog, that sounds like a good time. I miss real Christmas cookies. The stuff they have here is that pre-packaged stuff."

"Well, you're going to love these," Holly said.

"Do you make them?" he asked, grinning.

"No," she said. "He does. I try to avoid burning things."

Gerard laughed.

"Well, that's all right then," he said.

As we made our way to the car I casually noticed as my mother took Holly's hand and squeezed it, smiling.

"Thank you," she said softly.

"Of course," Holly said. "It's Christmas."

Chapter Seventy-Two

Holly

It should have been nerve-wracking having Gloria in the kitchen with me while I prepared dinner. Yet, for the life of me, I wasn't nervous and was instead having a great time. Gloria sat at the little kitchen table, a glass of wine on one side of her and the pie crust in front of her. I kept finding myself looking over my shoulder to watch her as she manipulated the dough and formed it into these amazing-looking pies. I was starting to understand where Lawson got it from.

After preparing dinner, we gathered her friends at the dinner table and settled in for a lovely Christmas meal. I found myself enjoying every second of it, to the point where my mind started wandering. Maybe this is what Christmas could be like from now on. Not just Christmas, either. All the major holidays.

Gloria was a wonderful woman and a lot of fun, with a wicked sense of humor. She kept cracking jokes at the table, keeping us all entertained and laughing. Her illness seemingly had no effect on her appetite, either, as she ate me under the table quickly. Even Lawson was impressed by it.

The other two seemed to fit in quickly and we chatted as we ate, each of them reminiscing on happy days and traditions they had with their families in years past. Some of those traditions sounded wonderful, and I started to secretly plan on incorporating them into my own. Hopefully we would do this again, and I could surprise them by bringing back their traditions for our celebration.

After we all finished eating, Gloria and I headed to the kitchen to bring out the pies. They were expertly baked, and while I should have felt jealous I could only admire her for them. Especially the pumpkin one, which I intended on eating with a mound of whipped cream.

Gerard avoided the pies in favor of cookies but everyone else dug in, bringing them into the main room, the lights dimmed, and eggnog and cocoa passed around with it. As the lights on the tree twinkled, Lawson put his arm around me and I saw Gloria smiling at us, then turn her attention back to the tree. My heart felt warm and the visions of potential holidays like this danced in my mind.

"I don't know about you," Samantha said after a long while, talking to Gloria, "but I think it's time we headed back. This has been wonderful, but I need to get to bed."

"Me, too," Gerard said. "Thank you for having us over, and for the cookies. But I'm beat."

"No worries," Lawson said. "I can bring you back. Let me get your coats."

"I'll come," I said.

"No, you don't have to do that," he said. "It's cold out there."

"I'd rather be cold with you than warm alone," I said.

Lawson smiled and stuffed his hat down over his head.

"Come on then, help me get their coats."

An hour later we were pulling back into the bed and breakfast, an empty car but full spirits. The snow was bright and reflecting a star-filled sky and large, full moon. We took our time walking in, taking in the beauty of our surroundings. As I opened the door I went to the kitchen, making us more cocoa and bringing it to him in the main room.

"I am going to miss drinking this stuff after the holidays," he said.

"You don't have to stop," I laughed. "They sell it all year."

"I know, but it doesn't mean anything unless it's after Thanksgiving and before New Year's," he said. "Any other time and it's just a warm drink. But at Christmas... it's magic."

We sat down on the couch together, not bothering with the TV and instead just listening to the fire as the tree twinkled and flashed softly. Lawson gently ran his fingers through my hair and kissed the top of my head as we sat there, and when I finished my cocoa I kissed his cheek and stood to bring the mug back to the kitchen. When I came back Lawson was standing by the tree, his hands behind his back.

"What's going on?" I asked.

"I have one more gift for you," he said.

"But we already opened our gifts," I said.

"I know," he said. "But this one was one I wanted to give you when we were alone."

"All right," I said suspiciously, walking over to him.

From behind him he pulled out a small box, wrapped in his signature haphazard style. I tore off the wrapping and then opened the box, gasping. Inside was a gorgeous stained-glass mistletoe. I looked up at him in surprise and then back down at it as it sparkled and shone in the firelight.

"This is beautiful," I said.

"I've been thinking a lot recently," he said. "About everything. About the future. About us."

My breath hitched as I realized we were finally going to have the talk I had been both looking forward to and dreading.

"Me, too," I said.

"So, I have to go back," he said, and I tried not to let him see how deflated just his saying that made me feel. "I have some loose ends to tie up and some agreements to sign. Contracts and that sort of thing. But then, after that, I'm coming back home. To Snowflake Hollow."

"You are?" I asked, my heart thumping in my chest.

"I found out my childhood home is going back on the market. The person who bought it decided to flip it and they did some renovations to it and are selling it. So, I'm buying it.

"Mom likes where she is, and she wants to stay there, but I like knowing that if she changes her mind she can always go home. I can take care of her there. She'll never have to worry about anything."

I felt like I could barely breathe. What he was saying was amazing, but there were still questions. Questions I needed answered.

"Where would you live?" I asked, forcing the words to come out of my mouth.

"I'm looking at another house that's nearby," he said. "But, if you didn't have any objection to it, I was thinking that I might spend most of my time here. With you." He motioned to the glass mistletoe in my hand. "Now that we have some permanent mistletoe, I am going to owe you an awful lot of kisses."

I laughed and he pulled me in tight for a kiss. I held the mistletoe above us as he did, and when he pulled back he saw it and laughed.

"See, it's already working," I said.

"Look, I know it's fast. Really fast. And if that means you need more time or more space, then you just say the word. But when I told you I loved you it might have been an accident to say it like that, but it wasn't an accident that I felt it. I'm in love with you, Holly White. Completely and hopelessly in love with you."

"I love you, too," I said, the words tumbling out of my mouth in relief to finally be given a voice. They had been sitting on the tip of my tongue for so long.

He grinned and took my hand, kissing my knuckles before using it to pull me tighter. Our foreheads rested on one another's, and we swayed a little as I looked at the mistletoe in my hand.

"You know, I guess this is what I had always been dreaming of. A White Christmas."

I groaned and he laughed at me.

"You had to," I said.

He nodded.

"I did," he said. "You know, you mentioned you were thinking about changing the name of the inn."

"I was," I said. "I don't know. I can't seem to think of anything I really like."

"Well, I really like the sound of Holly Lane."

The smile crept across my face slowly and I bit my bottom lip as he scooped me into his arms. I rested my cheek on his chest and my eyes flickered open to the tree with all its lights. I listened to his heartbeat for a moment as my eyes wandered over the tree, finally settling on one of my grandmother's ornaments.

It was one of the ones I loved the most. Shiny and glass, it reflected the lights so beautifully. It was intricately made and shaped like a diamond and hung from the center of the tree. I loved that ornament, but at the moment I felt like it was something more than just glass on a tree. The way the light reflected off of it, it was like it was winking at me.

Like my grandmother was winking at me.

It was in that moment, in Lawson's arms, that I realized I finally really was home for Christmas.

THE END

Snowflake
HOLLOW
12 DAYS OF CHRISTMAS
COMPLETE SERIES
USA TODAY BESTSELLING AUTHOR
LEXY TIMMS

Find Lexy Timms:

LEXY TIMMS NEWSLETTER:
http://www.lexytimms/newsletter
Lexy Timms Facebook Page:
https://www.facebook.com/SavingForever
Lexy Timms Website:
http://www.lexytimms.com

Want

FREE READS?

Sign up for Lexy Timms' newsletter
And she'll send you updates on new releases,
ARC copies of books and a whole lotta fun!

Sign up for news and updates!
http://www.lexytimms/newsletter

Holiday Romance by Lexy Timms

LOVERS IN LONDON SERIES #6
Sparkling
CHRISTMAS
USA TODAY BESTSELLING AUTHOR
LEXY TIMMS

DRIVING HOME FOR
Christmas
LEXY TIMMS
LIMITED
TIME
Lexy
Timms
FREE
DOWNLOAD

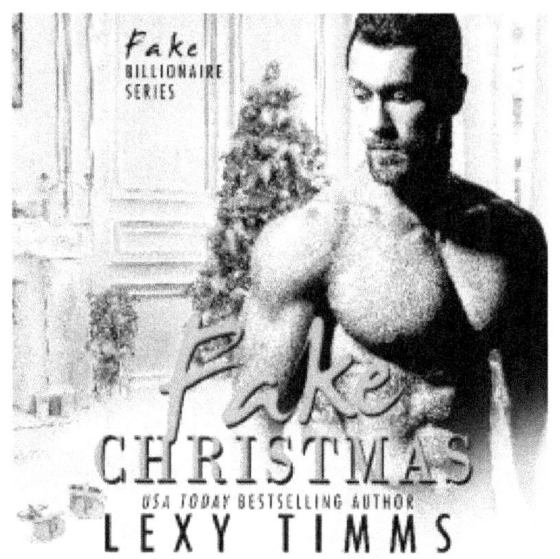
Fake
BILLIONAIRE
SERIES
Fake
CHRISTMAS
USA TODAY BESTSELLING AUTHOR
LEXY TIMMS

BUTLER &
HEIRESS
SERIES
All
Wrapped
Up
USA TODAY BESTSELLING AUTHOR
LEXY TIMMS

Don't miss out!

Visit the website below and you can sign up to receive emails whenever Lexy Timms publishes a new book. There's no charge and no obligation.

https://books2read.com/r/B-A-NNL-TSZTB

BOOKS 2 READ

Connecting independent readers to independent writers.

Did you love *Snowflake Hollow - Part 12*? Then you should read *Perfect Stranger*[1] by Lexy Timms!

In that perfect stranger, I found my fairytale...

Olivia Cadwell, brilliant with numbers but still having trouble figuring out where she fits into the world, is on the run from her hometown, courtesy of her mother's boyfriend—who has decided that Olivia is his next target.

Leo Folley, head of the multi-billion-dollar company his father started, is minding his own business and carrying on as usual... until his publicist gives him a deadline: Find a girlfriend, play nice with the press, and be a better face for the company, or the board is going to make trouble.

When Leo finds Olivia sleeping in her car in the alley outside of his office, he sees the perfect answer to his dilemma: a girl who needs mon-

---

1. https://books2read.com/u/47NKRR

2. https://books2read.com/u/47NKRR

ey and a place to stay in exchange for playing his date for the big charity auction. For Olivia, it's the perfect solution: money, a place to stay, and safety from the man she's sure is searching for her. What's not to love?

They both believe they can get through the week without taking anything too seriously.

They're both wrong.

A job is a job, until you're the boss' pretty woman...

The Millionaire's Pretty Woman Series

Book 1 – Perfect Stranger

Book 2 – Captive Devotion

Book 3 – Sweet Temptations

Read more at www.lexytimms.com.

Also by Lexy Timms

12 Days of Christmas
Snowflake Hollow - Part 1
Snowflake Hollow - Part 2
Snowflake Hollow - Part 3
Snowflake Hollow - Part 4
Snowflake Hollow - Part 5
Snowflake Hollow - Part 6
Snowflake Hollow - Part 7
Snowflake Hollow - Part 8
Snowflake Hollow - Part 9
Snowflake Hollow - Part 10
Snowflake Hollow - Part 11
Snowflake Hollow - Part 12

A Bad Boy Bullied Romance
I Hate You
I Hate You A Little Bit
I Hate You A Little Bit More

A Bump in the Road Series

Expecting Love
Selfless Act
Doctor's Orders

A Burning Love Series
Spark of Passion
Flame of Desire
Blaze of Ecstasy

A Chance at Forever Series
Forever Perfect
Forever Desired
Forever Together

A Dark Mafia Romance Series
Taken By The Mob Boss
Truce With The Mob Boss
Taking Over the Mob Boss
Trouble For The Mob Boss
Tailored By The Mob Boss
Tricking the Mob Boss

A Dating App Series
I've Been Matched
You've Been Matched
We've Been Matched

A "Kind of" Billionaire
Taking a Risk
Safety in Numbers
Pretend You're Mine

A Maybe Series
Maybe I Should
Maybe I Shouldn't
Maybe I Did

Assisting the Boss Series
Billion Reasons
Duke of Delegation
Late Night Meetings
Delegating Love
Suitors and Admirers

BBW Romance Series
Capturing Her Beauty
Pursuing Her Dreams
Tracing Her Curves

Beating the Biker Series
Making Her His

Making the Break
Making of Them

Betrayal at the Bay Series
Devil's Bay
Devil's Deceit
Devil's Duplicity

Billionaire Banker Series
Banking on Him
Price of Passion
Investing in Love
Knowing Your Worth
Treasured Forever
Banking on Christmas
Billionaire Banker Box Set Books #1-3

Billionaire CEO Brothers
Tempting the Player
Late Night Boardroom
Reviewing the Perfomance
Result of Passion
Directing the Next Move
Touching the Assets

Billionaire Hitman Series

The Hit
The Job
The Run

Billionaire Holiday Romance Series
Driving Home for Christmas
The Valentine Getaway
Cruising Love
Billionaire Holiday Romance Box Set

Billionaire in Disguise Series
Facade
Illusion
Charade

Billionaire Secrets Series
The Secret
Freedom
Courage
Trust
Impulse
Billionaire Secrets Box Set Books #1-3

Blind Sight Series
See Me
Fix Me

Eyes On Me

Branded Series
Money or Nothing
What People Say
Give and Take

Building Billions
Building Billions - Part 1
Building Billions - Part 2
Building Billions - Part 3

Butler & Heiress Series
To Serve
For Duty
No Chore
All Wrapped Up

Change of Heart Series
The Heart Needs
The Heart Wants
The Heart Knows

Counting the Billions
Counting the Days

Counting On You

Counting the Kisses

Cry Wolf Reverse Harem Series

Beautiful & Wild

Misunderstood

Never Tamed

Darkest Night Series

Savage

Vicious

Brutal

Sinful

Fierce

Diamond in the Rough Anthology

Billionaire Rock

Billionaire Rock - part 2

Dirty Little Taboo Series

Flirting Touch

Denying Pleasure

Forbidding Desire

Craving Passion

Dominating PA Series
Her Personal Assistant - Part 1
Her Personal Assistant - Part 2
Her Personal Assistant Box Set

Fake Billionaire Series
Faking It
Temporary CEO
Caught in the Act
Never Tell A Lie
Fake Christmas
Fake Billionaire Box Set #1-3

Firehouse Romance Series
Caught in Flames
Burning With Desire
Craving the Heat
Firehouse Romance Complete Collection

Forging Billions Series
Dirty Money
Petty Cash
Payment Required

For His Pleasure
Elizabeth
Georgia
Madison

Fortune Riders MC Series
Billionaire Biker
Billionaire Ransom
Billionaire Misery
Fortune Riders Box Set - Books #1-3

Fragile Series
Fragile Touch
Fragile Kiss
Fragile Love

Great Temptation Series
The Devil's Footsteps
Heaven's Command
Mortals Surrender

Hades' Spawn Motorcycle Club
One You Can't Forget
One That Got Away

One That Came Back
One You Never Leave
One Christmas Night
Hades' Spawn MC Complete Series

Hard Rocked Series
Rhyme
Harmony
Lyrics

Heart of Stone Series
The Protector
The Guardian
The Warrior

Heart of the Battle Series
Celtic Viking
Celtic Rune
Celtic Mann
Heart of the Battle Series Box Set

Heistdom Series
Master Thief
Goldmine
Diamond Heist
Smile For Me

Your Move
Green With Envy
Saving Money

Highlander Wolf Series
Pack Run
Pack Land
Pack Rules

Hollyweird Fae Series
Inception of Gold
Disruption of Magic
Guardians of Twilight

How To Love A Spy
The Secret
The Secret Life
The Secret Wife

Just About Series
About Love
About Truth
About Forever
Just About Box Set Books #1-3

Justice Series
Seeking Justice
Finding Justice
Chasing Justice
Pursuing Justice
Justice - Complete Series

Karma Series
Walk Away
Make Him Pay
Perfect Revenge

Kissed by Billions
Kissed by Passion
Kissed by Desire
Kissed by Love

Leaning Towards Trouble
Trouble
Discord
Tenacity

Love on the Sea Series
Ships Ahoy

Rough Sea
High Tide

Lovers in London Series
Risking Millions
Venture Capital
Worth the Expense
The Price of Luxury
Exclusive Passion
Lovers in London - 3 Book Box Set

Love You Series
Love Life
Need Love
My Love

Managing the Billionaire
Never Enough
Worth the Cost
Secret Admirers
Chasing Affection
Pressing Romance
Timeless Memories
Managing the Billionaire Box Set Books #1-3

Managing the Bosses Series

The Boss
The Boss Too
Who's the Boss Now
Love the Boss
I Do the Boss
Wife to the Boss
Employed by the Boss
Brother to the Boss
Senior Advisor to the Boss
Forever the Boss
Christmas With the Boss
Billionaire in Control
Billionaire Makes Millions
Billionaire at Work
Precious Little Thing
Priceless Love
Valentine Love
The Cost of Freedom
Trick or Treat
The Night Before Christmas
Gift for the Boss - Novella 3.5
Managing the Bosses Box Set #1-3
Managing the Bosses Novellas

Mislead by the Bad Boy Series
Deceived
Provoked
Betrayed

Model Mayhem Series

Shameless
Modesty
Imperfection

Moment in Time
Highlander's Bride
Victorian Bride
Modern Day Bride
A Royal Bride
Forever the Bride

Mountain Millionaire Series
Close to the Ridge
Crossing the Bluff
Climbing the Mount

My Best Friend's Sister
Hometown Calling
A Perfect Moment
Thrown in Together

My Darker Side Series
Darkest Hour
Time to Stop
Against the Light

Neverending Dream Series
Neverending Dream - Part 1
Neverending Dream - Part 2
Neverending Dream - Part 3
Neverending Dream - Part 4
Neverending Dream - Part 5
Neverending Dream Box Set Books #1-3

Outside the Octagon
Submit
Fight
Knockout

Protecting Diana Series
Her Bodyguard
Her Defender
Her Champion
Her Protector
Her Forever
Protecting Diana Box Set Books #1-3

Protecting Layla Series
His Mission
His Objective
His Devotion

Racing Hearts Series
Rush
Pace
Fast

Regency Romance Series
The Duchess Scandal - Part 1
The Duchess Scandal - Part 2

Reverse Harem Series
Primals
Archaic
Unitary

Roommate Wanted Series
The Roommate

R&S Rich and Single Series
Alex Reid
Parker
Sebastian

Saving Forever

Saving Forever - Part 1
Saving Forever - Part 2
Saving Forever - Part 3
Saving Forever - Part 4
Saving Forever - Part 5
Saving Forever - Part 6
Saving Forever Part 7
Saving Forever - Part 8
Saving Forever Boxset Books #1-3

Secrets & Lies Series
Strange Secrets
Evading Secrets
Inspiring Secrets
Lies and Secrets
Mastering Secrets
Alluring Secrets
Secrets & Lies Box Set Books #1-3

Shifting Desires Series
Jungle Heat
Jungle Fever
Jungle Blaze

Sin Series
Payment for Sin
Atonement Within
Declaration of Love

Southern Romance Series
Little Love Affair
Siege of the Heart
Freedom Forever
Soldier's Fortune

Spanked Series
Passion
Playmate
Pleasure

Spelling Love Series
The Author
The Book Boyfriend
The Words of Love

Strength & Style
Suits You, Sir
Tailor Made
Perfect Gentleman

Taboo Wedding Series
He Loves Me Not
With This Ring

Happily Ever After

Tattooist Series
Confession of a Tattooist
Surrender of a Tattooist
Heart of a Tattooist
Hopes & Dreams of a Tattooist

Tennessee Romance
Whisky Lullaby
Whisky Melody
Whisky Harmony

The Bad Boy Alpha Club
Battle Lines - Part 1
Battle Lines

The Brush Of Love Series
Every Night
Every Day
Every Time
Every Way
Every Touch
The Brush of Love Series Box Set Books #1-3

The City of Mayhem Series
True Mayhem
Relentless Chaos
Broken Disorder

The Debt
The Debt: Part 1 - Damn Horse
The Debt: Complete Collection

The Fire Inside Series
Dare Me
Defy Me
Burn Me

The Gentleman's Club Series
Gambler
Player
Wager

The Golden Game
On The Pitch
Respect the Game
All Game
Sweat and Tears

The Final Score

The Golden Mail
Hot Off the Press
Extra! Extra!
Read All About It
Stop the Press
Breaking News
This Just In
The Golden Mail Box Set Books #1-3

The Lucky Billionaire Series
Lucky Break
Streak of Luck
Lucky in Love

The Millionaire's Pretty Woman Series
Perfect Stranger
Captive Devotion
Sweet Temptations

The Sound of Breaking Hearts Series
Disruption
Destroy
Devoted

The University of Gatica Series
The Recruiting Trip
Faster
Higher
Stronger
Dominate
No Rush
University of Gatica - The Complete Series

T.N.T. Series
Troubled Nate Thomas - Part 1
Troubled Nate Thomas - Part 2
Troubled Nate Thomas - Part 3

Toxic Touch Series
Noxious
Lethal
Willful
Tainted
Craved
Toxic Touch Box Set Books #1-3

Undercover Boss Series
Marketing
Finance
Legal

Undercover Series
Perfect For Me
Perfect For You
Perfect For Us

Unknown Identity Series
Unknown
Unpublished
Unexposed
Unsure
Unwritten
Unknown Identity Box Set: Books #1-3

Unlucky Series
Unlucky in Love
UnWanted
UnLoved Forever

War Torn Letters Series
My Sweetheart
My Darling
My Beloved

Wet & Wild Series

Stormy Love
Savage Love
Secure Love

Worth It Series
Worth Billions
Worth Every Cent
Worth More Than Money

You & Me - A Bad Boy Romance
Just Me
Touch Me
Kiss Me

Standalone
Wash
Loving Charity
Summer Lovin'
Love & College
Billionaire Heart
First Love
Frisky and Fun Romance Box Collection
Beating Hades' Bikers
Everyone Loves a Bad Boy
Dead of Night

Watch for more at www.lexytimms.com.

About the Author

"Love should be something that lasts forever, not is lost forever." Visit USA TODAY BESTSELLING AUTHOR, LEXY TIMMS https://www.facebook.com/SavingForever *Please feel free to connect with me and share your comments. I love connecting with my readers.* Sign up for news and updates and freebies - I like spoiling my readers! http://eepurl.com/9i0vD website: www.lexytimms.com Dealing in Antique Jewelry and hanging out with her awesome hubby and three kids, Lexy Timms loves writing in her free time. MANAGING THE BOSS-ES is a bestselling 10-part series dipping into the lives of Alex Reid and Jamie Connors. Can a secretary really fall for her billionaire boss?

Read more at www.lexytimms.com.